THIRD-GRADE DETECTIVES #3

The Mystery
of the
Hairy Tomatoes

THIRD-GRADE DETECTIVES #3

The Mystery of the Hairy Tomatoes

by
George E. Stanley
illustrated by
Salvatore Murdocca

SCHOLASTIC INC.
New York Toronto London Auckland Sydney
Mexico City New Delhi Hong Kong Buenos Aires

This book is dedicated to the wonderful students in Mrs. Schlueter's third-grade class at Lincoln Elementary School in Norman, Oklahoma. You're great! Thanks for all your help.

ISBN 0-439-41290-0

12 11 10 9 8 7 6 5   4 5 6 7/0

Printed in the U.S.A.   40

First Scholastic printing, September 2002

Designed by Steve Scott.
The text for this book was set in 12-point Lino Letter.

Chapter One

Noelle Trocoderro raised her hand.

"Yes, Noelle?" Mr. Merlin said.

"The police tried to arrest my dog, Rover, last night," Noelle said.

Mr. Merlin looked puzzled. "Why?"

"They said he tore up some of Mrs. Ruston's tomato plants," Noelle said.

"But Rover didn't do it. He had an alibi. He was asleep in my room when it happened."

"Oh, yes, I heard about the tomato plants this morning," Mr. Merlin said. "But I didn't know that Rover was a suspect in the crime."

Noelle nodded.

Then Mr. Merlin told the rest of the class what had happened.

Mrs. Ruston was one of the fifth-grade teachers at their school.

She and her husband owned a small farm at the edge of town.

They grew vegetables to sell to the local grocery stores.

They were famous for their tomatoes.

During the night, somebody had torn up several of the tomato plants.

Mrs. Ruston said it looked like a dog had been digging around in them.

"The police are investigating it," Mr. Merlin said. He looked at Noelle. "Why would Mrs. Ruston think that Rover did it?"

"He tore up some of her flowers last month," Noelle said. "She's still mad at him because of that."

Todd Sloan raised his hand.

"Could we help the police solve the mystery, Mr. Merlin?" he asked. "Could we find the dog that did it?"

"That's a good idea, Mr. Merlin," Noelle said. "If we could find the real dog, then Mrs. Ruston would know that Rover didn't do it."

"I'm sure the police would appreciate any help the Third-Grade Detectives could give them," Mr. Merlin said.

Amber Lee raised her hand.

"Yes, Amber Lee?" Mr. Merlin said.

"I bought a pretty greeting card for Preston Edwards," Amber Lee said. "I want everybody to sign it."

"Who's Preston Edwards?" Leon Dennis asked.

"He's that new kid with long, blond hair," Todd said. "He's in the other third-grade class."

"He just moved across the street from me," Amber Lee said.

"And he's really nervous about going to a new school.

"He doesn't know if the kids here will like him.

"So I want to make him feel welcome.

"That's why I bought him this card. It says: 'We're glad you're here.'"

"Amber Lee has a boyfriend!" Leon sang. "Amber Lee has a boyfriend!"

"I do not!" Amber Lee cried.

"That's enough, Leon," Mr. Merlin said.

He turned to Amber Lee.

3

"I think it was nice of you to get Preston a card, Amber Lee," he said. "Yes, you may let everyone sign it."

Amber Lee began passing the card around the room.

Johnny Fowler raised his hand. "How do we start to solve the mystery, Mr. Merlin?" he asked.

Noelle raised her hand.

"I know! I know!" she said.

"Okay, Noelle," Mr. Merlin said. "Tell us."

"We go to Mrs. Ruston's farm," Noelle said.

"That's the scene of the crime.

"We look for evidence there."

"What kind of evidence?" Johnny asked.

Noelle didn't know what kind of evidence they were supposed to look for.

Why did Johnny have to ask her a question she couldn't answer?

Now she wished she hadn't even raised her hand.

She looked over at Mr. Merlin.

"I'm going to give you a secret code clue," Mr. Merlin said. "It'll tell you what kind of evidence to look for."

He turned around.

He started writing on the chalkboard.

He wrote:

OLLP ULI HLNVGSRMT GSZG GSV
HFHKVXG OVUG YVSRMW

Noelle knew that Johnny was looking at her.

She knew he expected her to solve the secret code clue so he'd know what evidence to look for.

She could tell he thought she was really smart.

She didn't want to disappoint him.

She looked at the secret code clue again.

Unfortunately, she had no idea what it meant.

And she knew Mr. Merlin wouldn't give them any rules for the secret code until they had tried to solve it without them.

He said that solving secret codes made them think better.

Noelle hoped she could find some evidence before someone else solved the secret code clue.

She didn't want Johnny to think she wasn't the smartest girl in the class after all.

Chapter Two

Noelle peeked out from behind the big tree next to the swings.

She saw Todd walking past her.

She ducked back behind the tree.

"Noelle! Noelle!" Todd shouted. "Where are you?"

"Shhh!" Noelle whispered. "Don't say my name so loud!"

"*Noelle?*" Todd whispered.

Noelle peeked out from behind the big tree again.

"What are you doing there?" Todd said. "I've been looking all over for you."

"Is she gone yet?" Noelle asked.

"Is *who* gone yet?" Todd said.

"Mrs. Ruston," Noelle replied. "Is she gone yet?"

Todd turned around.

"I don't see her," he said. "She must be on the other side of the building."

Noelle stepped out from behind the tree.

"I had to hide from her," she said.

"She won't leave me alone.

"She keeps asking me all these questions about Rover.

"She still thinks he tore up her tomato plants."

Noelle looked at Todd.

"I'm sure she's planning to kidnap him this time!"

"Really?" Todd said.

Noelle nodded.

"You know she's never liked him," she said. "She's been trying to get rid of him for years."

"I know," Todd said.

Noelle looked around to see if anyone else was listening.

"She wants to know *when* I take him for a walk," she whispered.

"And she wants to know *where*.

"She's probably going to ambush us some- where along the way."

"Do you really think she'd do something like that, Noelle?" Todd said.

"Yes, Todd! She's under a lot of stress!" Noelle said. "People under a lot of stress do weird things."

"You're right," Todd said. "That happens to my parents sometimes."

"Have you solved the secret code clue yet?" Noelle asked.

Todd nodded.

"You have?" Noelle cried. "Why didn't you tell me?"

"I couldn't find you," Todd said.

"You've found me now," Noelle said. "So tell me what it is."

"Well, since Mr. Merlin started giving us secret code clues to solve, I've been reading a lot about codes," Todd said. "This one is a reverse alphabet code."

"What does that mean?" Noelle said.

"I'll show you," Todd said.

He picked up a stick.

In the dirt, he printed all the letters of the alphabet in a row.

Underneath those letters, he printed the alphabet *backward*.

"In this secret code, *A* is *Z, B* is *Y, C* is *X* and so on," Todd said.

"The secret code clue is:

OLLP ULI HLNVGSRMT GSZG GSV HFHKVXG OVUG YVSRMW.

"To solve it, you find the letter in the secret code in the second line, then you look above it."

"Let me do it!" Noelle said.

"Okay," Todd said.

"*O* is *L, L* is *O,* so that's two O's, and *P* is *K.* "*Look!*" Noelle cried.

Todd nodded.

Noelle found the letters for the rest of the secret code clue. "*Look for something that the suspect left behind!*" she said.

"Right," Todd said.

Noelle thought for a minute. "Of course!" she cried. "Mr. Merlin wants us to look for something that the dog left behind *at the scene of the crime!*"

"What would the dog leave behind at Mrs. Ruston's farm?" Todd said.

Noelle shrugged.

"It could be anything.

"A collar. A leash. A dog tag.

"If we can find *something* there that belongs to the other dog, then Mrs. Ruston will have to believe that Rover didn't tear up her tomato plants!"

The bell to end recess rang.

Noelle and Todd hurried toward the door to Mr. Merlin's classroom.

"We'll go to Mrs. Ruston's farm tonight," Noelle whispered.

Chapter Three

After dinner, Noelle and Todd got on their bicycles.

They headed for the public library.

There were still lots of people on the streets.

And it was well lit all the way.

Noelle was glad she lived in a small town.

Her cousin Jane, who lived in a city, was never allowed to ride her bicycle very far from home.

Noelle had a plan all worked out.

They'd get their library books.

Then they'd ride their bicycles over to the Rustons' farm.

Noelle's parents knew she liked to take her time at the library.

So if they hurried up and checked out their books, they could make it to the farm and be back home before anyone got worried.

They should have plenty of time to look for something the dog left behind in the tomato patch.

"I brought a plastic bag," Noelle said. "Did you bring your flashlight?"

Todd nodded.

Noelle was really excited.

This was the first mystery where they could act like real detectives.

She had seen a lot of shows on television where detectives used a flashlight at night to look for evidence. When they found it, they put it inside a plastic bag to keep it safe.

Noelle and Todd finally got to the library.

They quickly found the books they wanted.

They handed them to Mrs. Charter, the librarian.

"What's your hurry?" Mrs. Charter asked.

"We have to help a friend," Noelle said. "He's in trouble."

Mrs. Charter looked concerned.

"Oh, I'm sorry to hear that," she said. "I hope you're able to help him."

"We will be if we find something the other dog left behind," Todd said.

Mrs. Charter looked surprised.

"The other dog?" she said. "What do you mean?"

"Oh, nothing," Noelle said.

She kicked Todd on the shin.

"Ouch!" Todd cried.

"Well, we need to go now," Noelle said. "Bye, Mrs. Charter!"

Noelle headed toward the door.

Todd was right behind her.

"What's wrong with you?" he said. "Why did you kick me?"

"I don't want Mrs. Charter to suspect what we're doing," she said. "She and Mrs. Ruston are good friends."

"Oh, yeah. She'd probably call Mrs. Ruston," Todd said. "And then Mrs. Ruston would be waiting for us at the farm."

"Exactly," Noelle said.

They strapped their books onto their bicycles.

Then they headed toward the Rustons' farm.

"It's darker here than I thought it would be," Noelle said when they got there.

15

"Yeah," Todd agreed. He looked around. "Where do we start?"

"We look for the place where that dog tore up the tomato plants," Noelle said.

Todd shone his flashlight over the tomato patch.

"I hope nobody sees us," he said. "We'll be in trouble for sure."

"We're not planning to tear up any tomato plants ourselves, Todd," Noelle said. "We're just looking for some evidence that Rover didn't commit the crime."

They slowly made their way through several rows of tomato plants.

"We have to be careful, though. Our footprints are everywhere," Noelle said. "If we step on one of these plants, Mrs. Ruston will know who did it."

Todd stopped. "I forgot about that."

"But I don't think anyone will notice our footprints if none of the plants are broken," Noelle said. "Just be careful."

Finally, they reached the middle of the tomato patch.

There were several broken plants.

"This is it, Noelle!" Todd said. "This is *the scene of the crime!*"

"Shine the flashlight around on the ground," Noelle said. "Look for something that the dog left behind."

But after several minutes, they still hadn't found anything.

"Maybe we need to get down on our hands and knees," Todd said. "Maybe it's something smaller than a collar or a leash or a dog tag."

"That's a good idea," Noelle said.

So they got down on their hands and knees and started crawling around.

"Hey, Todd!" Noelle whispered. "Look at this!"

Todd looked. "What is it?"

"Hairs!" Noelle whispered. "*Two long, yellow hairs!*"

"Do you think they belong to the other dog?" Todd asked.

"I'm sure they do," Noelle said.

"Well, Rover's hair is short and black!" Todd said. "So that proves he didn't tear up the tomato plants!"

"That's what I think, too," Noelle said.

"Let's show them to Mrs. Ruston," Todd said. "Then she'll know Rover didn't do it."

"I don't think that's a good idea," Noelle said.

"Why not?" Todd said.

"She might say *we planted the evidence*," Noelle said. "She might say we put the hairs here ourselves."

"You're right," Todd said. "But what do we do now?"

Noelle picked up the hairs and put them inside the plastic bag.

"We need to find a dog with long, yellow hair," Noelle said. "Then we'll have the real criminal."

Chapter Four

The next morning at school, Noelle and Todd told Mr. Merlin that they had solved the secret code clue.

They showed him the long, yellow hairs they had found in the tomato patch.

"Rover couldn't have done it," Noelle explained. "He has short, black hair. We need to find a dog with long, yellow hair."

"I know two dogs with long, yellow hair. George and June Bug," Amber Lee said. "They're awful dogs. I think they could both be guilty."

"Where do they live?" Todd asked.

"They live across the street from me," Amber Lee said. "They don't like me, either."

"I don't think they could have done it," Todd said.

Noelle looked at him. "Why not?"

"Our town has leash laws," Todd said.

"The police are always looking for stray dogs.

"They didn't find one after Mrs. Ruston called them.

"I think they would have picked up George and June Bug before they got to the farm.

"I think we need to look for a dog with long, yellow hair that lives closer to Mrs. Ruston's farm.

"I think whoever did this got in and out before anyone could catch him."

"That's true," Noelle said.

"Well, I'm proud of all of you. You're really thinking a lot about this mystery," Mr. Merlin said, "but I'm going to give you another secret code clue."

Noelle knew what that meant.

No matter how good Mr. Merlin said they were doing, he gave them secret code clues to make sure they stayed on track.

Mr. Merlin turned around.

He started writing on the chalkboard.

He wrote:

NER GUR LRYYBJ UNVEF ERNYYL QBT UNVEF?

"Why don't you work on this for a few minutes?" Mr. Merlin said. "It's something else you need to think about."

The class started trying to solve the secret code clue.

Noelle was glad that Todd had showed her how to solve the other one.

She hoped this was the same type of code.

She wrote the alphabet across the top of a piece of paper.

Underneath, she wrote the alphabet backward.

She tried to solve the secret code clue.

But none of the words made sense.

She looked over at Todd. He was shaking his head.

Noelle knew he hadn't solved it, either.

It wasn't the same secret code.

Well, she'd just start looking for a dog with long, yellow hair that lived close to Mrs. Ruston's farm.

If she could find him, she knew she could solve the mystery.

They did spelling.

Then they did math.

Finally, the recess bell rang.

Noelle and Todd headed for the swings.

"How can we find a dog with long, yellow hair that lives near Mrs. Ruston's farm?" Todd asked.

Noelle was pumping high into the air on a swing.

She loved the feeling it gave her.

Now she could see the roof of the school building.

"I'm still thinking about it," she shouted to Todd. "There has to be a way."

Suddenly, Noelle stopped swinging.

"I know how to do it!" she said.

Todd stopped swinging, too.

"How?" he asked.

Noelle grinned. "It's easy!" she said. "We'll just ask all the people who live around there if they know a dog with long, yellow hair!"

After school, Noelle and Todd rode over to the neighborhood by Mrs. Ruston's farm.

They parked their bicycles in front of the first house.

They went up to the door.

They knocked.

An elderly woman answered.

She was holding two cats.

"Do you have a dog with long, yellow hair?" Noelle asked her.

The woman shook her head. "No dogs here," she said.

They thanked the woman and walked their bicycles to the next house.

They kept asking until they got to the last house.

In the backyard, they saw a dog with long, yellow hair.

"That has to be the one," Noelle whispered. "But he looks too nice to do something mean like tearing up Mrs. Ruston's tomato plants."

"That's probably how he gets away with it," Todd said.

"He must know a way to get out of the backyard.

"And then he only has to go a few feet to the tomato patch."

Todd looked over at Noelle.

"What do we do now?" he asked.

"We do what Dr. Smiley would do," Noelle said. "We get some evidence."

Dr. Smiley was Mr. Merlin's friend.

She was a policewoman who used science to solve crimes.

She was also a good friend of Mr. Merlin's Third-Grade Detectives.

She had helped them solve several of their mysteries.

Noelle and Todd walked up to the front door.

They rang the bell.

A man answered.

He didn't look very friendly.

"What do you want?" he demanded.

"We're working on a school project," Noelle said. "Would you give us some of your dog's hairs?"

"Silly kids!" the man said.

He slammed the door.

Noelle looked at Todd. "We have to get some of that dog's hairs," she said.

"That way Dr. Smiley could look at them under the microscope.

"I'm sure she could tell us if the hairs we found in the tomato patch belong to the dog in this man's backyard."

Suddenly, they heard a noise at the side of the house.

They hurried off the front porch.

The man was backing his car out of the driveway.

The dog with the long, yellow hair was sitting in the front seat. He was looking out the window at them.

Noelle thought he had a friendly face.

She sighed. "We'll never get any hairs off that dog," she said.

"I guess we'll just have to solve the secret code clue," Todd said. "Maybe it'll tell us what to do next."

Chapter Five

The next morning, Todd and Noelle walked to school.

"We have to do something fast," Noelle said. "Mrs. Ruston was walking by my house early this morning."

"She lives just down the street from us, Noelle," Todd said. "Maybe she was getting some exercise."

Noelle shook her head.

"She kept walking back and forth, Todd," she said.

"She kept looking at my house.

"I think she was trying to decide whether she should kidnap Rover or not."

"I wonder what they do to teachers who kidnap pets," Todd said.

"I don't know," Noelle said. "I've never heard of it happening before."

When they got to school, Noelle told Mr. Merlin that she and Todd had found a dog with long yellow hair.

"He lives near Mrs. Ruston's farm," she said.

"I'm positive he's the dog who tore up Mrs. Ruston's tomato plants."

"The man who owns the dog acted really suspicious, too," Todd said.

"When we asked him if we could have some hairs from his dog, he put the dog in his car and drove away."

"That sounds suspicious to me," Amber Lee said.

Mr. Merlin smiled.

"Has anyone solved the secret code clue yet?" he asked.

No one had.

"Then I'll give you some rules," Mr. Merlin said.

He turned around.

He started writing on the chalkboard.

He wrote:

1. Split the alphabet.

2. Start in the middle with the beginning.

Noelle looked at the rules.

Sometimes she thought Mr. Merlin's rules were harder than his secret codes.

Amber Lee raised her hand.

"Yes, Amber Lee?" Mr. Merlin said.

"I'm sending Preston Edwards another greeting card," Amber Lee said. "May I have the class sign it?"

Leon rolled his eyes. "Amber Lee loves Preston!" he sang. "Amber Lee loves Preston!"

"Leon!" Mr. Merlin said. "That's enough!"

He turned to Amber Lee.

"Yes, you may have the class sign the card," he said. "Does Preston like our school?"

"Sort of," Amber Lee said. She sighed. "But he's still under a lot of stress."

Amber Lee took the card to each person's desk and let him or her sign it.

Then the class worked on spelling and math.

When the lunch bell rang, Noelle and Todd headed to the cafeteria.

"Have you figured out the secret code clue yet?" Noelle whispered to Todd.

Todd shook his head.

"I thought you said you'd been studying secret codes," Noelle said.

"This one has me stumped," Todd said.

They got their silverware and trays.

Then they got in line.

"Please don't put any tomatoes on my hamburger," Todd told the server. "I don't like tomatoes."

"Me, either," Noelle said.

"I'd like extras, please!"

Noelle and Todd turned.

Amber Lee was standing in line behind them.

She gave them a silly grin.

"I keep one for my hamburger," she said.

"I give the others to Preston.

"He loves tomatoes."

Todd and Noelle picked up their trays.

They found a table and sat at one end.

Amber Lee sat at the other end.

Noelle saw Amber Lee motioning for someone to come over to where she was sitting.

Noelle turned around.

She saw Preston Edwards heading toward Amber Lee.

When Preston reached the table, he leaned down so Amber Lee could whisper something in his ear.

When Amber Lee finished whispering, she handed him the greeting card that everybody had signed.

She also gave him two of her tomatoes.

Noelle heard him say thank you.

Then Preston went back to his table.

"I think Leon's right," Noelle said. "I think Amber Lee likes Preston a lot."

She took a bite of her hamburger.

Suddenly, Amber Lee screamed.

Everyone looked at her.

She was pointing to her hamburger.

"There's a hair on my tomato!" she cried.

Chapter Six

"I have to get that hair!" Noelle whispered to Todd.

"Why?" Todd asked.

"More evidence. It could belong to that dog who tore up Mrs. Ruston's tomato plants," Noelle said, still whispering. "Maybe the cooks didn't wash the tomatoes very well today."

"Oh, yuck!" Todd said. "I think I'm going to be sick!"

Noelle pushed her way into the crowd of people now surrounding Amber Lee.

She leaned down close to the slice of tomato on Amber Lee's hamburger.

A long, yellow hair was lying on top of it.

Noelle reached out and picked it up with her fingers.

Then she backed out of the crowd.

She bumped into Mrs. Ruston.

Mrs. Ruston gave her a suspicious look.

Noelle held her breath.

But Mrs. Ruston didn't say anything to her.

Noelle just turned and pushed her way through the crowd.

"I was right!" Noelle whispered to Todd. She showed him the long, yellow hair. "It belongs to that dog!"

Noelle wrapped the hair inside a paper napkin.

"I can't believe the cooks didn't wash the tomatoes," Todd said. "I wonder what else they left in our food today?"

"I don't want to know," Noelle said.

"Where's a hair?" Mrs. Ruston shouted. "I don't see any hair!"

"Well, there was one here just a minute ago!" Amber Lee shouted. "What happened to it?"

"Do you think we should have left the hair on the tomato?" Todd whispered. "Maybe we should have let Mrs. Ruston see it there."

Noelle thought about that for a minute.

She wondered if Todd was right.

"Well, it's too late now," she said. "Mrs. Ruston would see me if I tried to put it back on the tomato."

"That's true," Todd said.

Noelle looked around the cafeteria.

Mrs. Jenkins, the principal, was running toward the crowd of people that had Amber Lee surrounded.

"Let's get out of here," Noelle said.

She and Todd left the cafeteria.

They went back to their classroom.

Mr. Merlin was eating an apple.

All the teachers took turns having cafeteria duty.

This wasn't Mr. Merlin's week to eat with the students.

"Have you solved the secret code clue?" Mr. Merlin asked.

"Not yet," Noelle said.

"You need to work on it," Mr. Merlin said. "You don't want to head your investigation in the wrong direction."

He went back to eating his apple.

Noelle looked at Todd.

"What did he mean by that?" she whispered.

"I think he's telling us that we're doing something wrong," Todd said.

So they worked on the secret code clue some more.

But by the time Mr. Merlin started class again, they still hadn't solved it.

When school was over, Noelle said, "We have to go back to that man's house. We have to get some hairs from his dog."

"What if the man won't let us have them?" Todd said.

"I'm not going to ask him," Noelle said. "I think I can get some through the fence."

She remembered how friendly the dog looked when they were there yesterday.

She doubted the man petted him much.

She was sure that if she was nice to the dog he would let her have some of his hairs.

She got a pair of tweezers and a plastic bag.

Then they rode their bicycles back to the man's house.

The man's car wasn't in the driveway.

But the dog was in the backyard.

"Let's hurry," Todd said. "I don't want that man to come home and see us doing this."

"If his dog doesn't mind, I don't think he should mind," Noelle said. "It's not his hairs we want."

Noelle squatted next to the fence.

The dog came up and licked her hand.

But when Noelle took out her tweezers, the dog moved away.

"Here, doggie, doggie!" Noelle said. "I'm not going to hurt you."

The dog came back to the fence.

It licked Noelle's hand again.

But when she tried to get some of his hairs, he ran to the middle of the backyard.

He started barking.

"Oh, great!" Noelle muttered. "He thinks it's a game."

"We have to get out of here," Todd said. "Everyone in the neighborhood will know what we're doing."

Noelle opened the back gate.

"What are you doing?" Todd said.

"I'm going to get some of his hairs," Noelle said.

"You said you could get them through the fence," Todd reminded her.

"I was wrong," Noelle said.

She went inside the backyard.

She started walking slowly toward the barking dog.

The dog stayed where he was, but he continued to bark.

When Noelle reached him, she squatted on her knees.

She took the tweezers out of her pocket.

Suddenly, the dog bounded off.

Noelle jumped up and began chasing him.

"Help me, Todd!" she shouted. "I can't do this by myself."

Noelle and Todd chased the dog around the yard for several minutes.

The dog was having a lot of fun.

Noelle was getting frustrated.

Finally, she and Todd cornered the dog.

But Noelle didn't have to use the tweezers.

Several tufts of the dog's hair came off in her hands.

She stuffed them inside the plastic bag.

The dog started barking again.

Noelle could tell he wanted to play some more.

"We can't play now," Noelle said. "We have to take your hair to Dr. Smiley."

Chapter Seven

They rode their bicycles to Dr. Smiley's house. She was just pulling into her driveway when they got there.

She waved to them.

Noelle thought Dr. Smiley was wonderful.

She always had time for Mr. Merlin's Third-Grade Detectives.

Noelle was sure that Dr. Smiley and Mr. Merlin were a couple.

But they never said anything about it.

Noelle thought they made a great couple.

She wondered if they'd get married one of these days.

Noelle was sure they'd ask her to be a flower girl.

"We're solving the new mystery, Dr. Smiley," Noelle said.

Dr. Smiley smiled. "I thought that's what you were doing," she said.

"We need to look at some hairs under the microscope," Todd said.

"That sounds interesting," Dr. Smiley said. "Come on inside."

Noelle and Todd followed Dr. Smiley into her house.

They went downstairs to her basement laboratory.

Noelle told her about the trouble at Mrs. Ruston's vegetable farm.

"She thinks Rover dug up some of the tomato plants," Noelle said.

"But Todd and I found two long, yellow hairs there.

"We found a long, yellow hair on Amber Lee's tomato in the cafeteria, too."

Dr. Smiley blinked. "You did?" she said.

Todd nodded. "The cafeteria cooks didn't wash the tomatoes very well today."

"So Rover couldn't have committed the crime," Noelle said. "Rover has short, black hair."

"We think we know which dog really did it, though," Todd continued. "He lives in a house near Mrs. Ruston's farm."

"And his owner isn't very friendly," Noelle said.

"But we went back there today and got some of the dog's hairs.

"We want to compare the hairs we found at the farm and on Amber Lee's tomato with the hairs from this dog.

"If they match, then we'll know for sure who the guilty dog is."

"That way Mrs. Ruston won't kidnap Rover," Todd added.

"Well, I'm very impressed by what you two have done so far," Dr. Smiley said. "You are very good at using science to solve crimes."

Dr. Smiley prepared the microscope.

She got out two glass slides.

Noelle gave her one of the hairs they had found in the tomato patch.

Then she gave her the hair they had found on Amber Lee's tomato.

Finally, she gave her one of the hairs they

had taken from the dog in the man's backyard.

Dr. Smiley lined them up on the glass slide.

She put the other glass slide on top of them.

She looked at the slide under the microscope.

Then she let Noelle and Todd look.

"What do you see?" Dr. Smiley asked.

"The first two hairs look alike," Noelle said. "The third hair looks different."

"That's correct," Dr. Smiley said.

Noelle was puzzled.

"Does that mean that the first two hairs didn't come from the dog in the man's back-yard?" she asked.

Dr. Smiley nodded.

"The dog you got the hairs from didn't leave hair in the tomato patch," she said.

"That wasn't his hair on Amber Lee's tomato, either."

Noelle sighed. "I thought we had solved the mystery," she said.

"What do we do now?" Todd asked.

"Don't give up," Dr. Smiley said. "You have the evidence right here."

Noelle looked at her. "We do?" she said.

"Yes, you do," Dr. Smiley said. "You're just not using it right."

"What do you mean?" Noelle said.

"Mr. Merlin told me about the secret code clue he gave you," Dr. Smiley said. "If you solve that, you'll know what to do with the evidence you have."

Chapter Eight

When they got to Todd's house, his grandmother said, "How about some peanut butter cookies and cold milk?"

"That sounds great," Todd said. "I think better if I'm eating."

"Me, too," Noelle said.

They sat down at the kitchen table.

They ate their cookies and drank their milk.

They thought about the secret code clue.

NER GUR LRYYBJ UNVEF ERNYYL QBT UNVEF.

They thought about the secret code clue rules.

Split the alphabet.

Start in the middle with the beginning.

Noelle took a sheet of paper.

She picked up a pencil.

She wrote the letters of the alphabet down the side of the paper.

Todd did the same thing.

Noelle looked at what she had written.

"Split the alphabet," she said. She thought for a minute. "If you split something, you break it in half, right?"

"Right," Todd said.

"That means we need to break the alphabet in half," Noelle said.

She drew a line between *M* and *N*.

"Now, then, the alphabet is split," she said.

"If you start in the middle with the beginning, then you . . ."

Noelle looked at what she had written.

"Oh, I know!" she cried.

"The first half of the alphabet is A to M.

"The second half of the alphabet is N to Z.

"If we start in the middle with the beginning, then we start at *N* and write *A* beside it."

Todd looked.

"Yes! Yes! That's it!" he said. "*O* would be *B, P* would be *C* and so on."

Noelle and Todd finished the rest of the alphabet.

Then they used it to solve the secret code clue.

"Are the yellow hairs really dog hairs?" Noelle said. She looked at Todd.

"Of course, they are," Todd said.

Noelle thought for a minute.

"Maybe they're not, Todd," she said.

"If they were, why would Mr. Merlin have this as a secret code clue?

"And why would Dr. Smiley say she'd wait until we solved it before she told us about the hairs under the microscope?"

"If they're not dog hairs, then what are they?" Todd said. *"Cat hairs?"*

"Cats don't dig like that," Noelle said.

"Well, what other animals dig like that, then?" Todd asked.

"Humans," Noelle replied.

Todd gasped. "You think a *person* did this?"

Noelle nodded.

"Who could it be?" Todd asked.

"That's what we have to find out," Noelle said.

"How do we do that?" Todd asked.

"We go back to Dr. Smiley's house," Noelle said.

"We find out for sure if the hair we found at the scene of the crime belongs to a person.

"If it does, then we start thinking about possible suspects."

They headed out the door.

They rode their bicycles back to Dr. Smiley's house.

When Dr. Smiley opened the front door, Noelle said, "We solved the secret code clue!"

"Are the yellow hairs really dog hairs?" Todd said.

"Now we don't think they are," Noelle said. "We think they're *human* hairs."

Dr. Smiley smiled.

"Good work!" she said. "Come on in."

She took them back down to the laboratory.

The slide with the three hairs was still under the microscope.

"Take another look," she said.

Noelle looked into the eyepiece of the microscope.

She saw the three hairs lined up together.

"Each hair has three layers," Dr. Smiley said.

"The cuticle, the cortex, and the medulla.

"The *cuticle* is the outer layer of hair.

"It protects the cortex and the medulla.

"The *cortex* determines the color of the hair.

"The *medulla* is a collection of cells in the center of the hair.

"These cells have a definite pattern.

"That helps determine whether the hair belongs to an animal or to a human.

"The hairs you found in the tomato patch and on Amber Lee's tomato belong to a human.

"And I think they belong to the same person.

"You need to look for someone with long, blond hair."

Noelle turned to Todd. "And who do we know with long, blond hair who likes tomatoes?"

Chapter Nine

"Preston Edwards!" Todd cried.

"Right!" Noelle said.

She turned to Dr. Smiley.

"But why would Preston leave some of his hairs at Mrs. Ruston's farm and on Amber Lee's tomato?" she asked.

"I'm sure he didn't do it on purpose," Dr. Smiley said. "It's a normal process."

"Hairs just fall off our bodies.

"And if people are really upset about something, they lose even more hairs.

"That's why criminals almost always leave some of their hairs at the scene of a crime.

"They're usually under a lot of stress."

"Amber Lee said Preston was upset about coming to a new school," Noelle said.

"Well, that could certainly be a reason that he lost some of his hairs," Dr. Smiley said.

"I'm never going to get upset about anything again," Noelle said. "I don't want to lose my hair."

"Me, either," Todd said.

Dr. Smiley smiled.

"I'm afraid you don't have much choice," she said.

Noelle shuddered. She didn't like the thought of her hair falling out all over the place.

"Well, now you have a suspect," Dr. Smiley said. "What do you need to do next?"

"We need to get a hair from Preston's head," Noelle said. "Then we can compare it to the hairs we found at Mrs. Ruston's farm and on Amber Lee's tomato."

"That's excellent police work, Noelle," Dr. Smiley said.

Noelle smiled at Dr. Smiley.

She liked it when Dr. Smiley paid her compliments.

She was sure she was going to be Dr. Smiley's best assistant in the police laboratory when she grew up.

Noelle and Todd thanked Dr. Smiley for her help.

Then they headed back to Todd's house.

"I know how we can get one of Preston's hairs," Noelle said.

"How?" Todd asked.

"You keep him busy tomorrow at recess," Noelle said, "and I'll slip up behind him with my tweezers and . . ."

"I don't think that's a good idea," Todd said.

So they thought about it some more.

"I know!" Todd said.

Noelle looked over at him. "What?"

"Tomorrow at lunch, we'll ask the servers to put double tomatoes on our hamburgers," Todd said.

"But I hate tomatoes," Noelle said.

"That doesn't matter," Todd said. "We're not going to eat them. We're going to give them to Preston."

Noelle looked puzzled.

"Here's how we'll do it," Todd continued.

"We'll get the tomatoes.

"We'll sit close to Preston.

"You'll say, 'I don't want these tomatoes.'

"Preston will hear you.

"He'll come over to our table.

"You'll tell him you want to whisper a secret.

"He'll lean over your plate.

"And some of his hair will fall onto your tomatoes!"

"Oh, that is so gross!" Noelle said. She thought about it for a minute. "But it might work."

"Of course, it'll work," Todd said.

The next day at school, Noelle could hardly keep her mind on spelling or math or reading.

When Mr. Merlin asked the class if anyone had solved the secret code clue, Noelle raised her hand.

"Don't tell," Todd whispered.

"We're supposed to tell, Todd," Noelle said. "Mr. Merlin said the Third-Grade Detectives have to work together."

"Well, don't tell that we think Preston did it," Todd said.

So Noelle told the class everything except

that she and Todd thought Preston Edwards had stolen the tomatoes from Mrs. Ruston's farm.

"And just as soon as we get a hair from this person's head, we'll solve the mystery," she concluded.

Amber Lee suddenly gasped. "Oh, no!"

"What's wrong, Amber Lee?" Mr. Merlin asked.

Amber Lee gave Noelle and Todd a dirty look.

"I need to go to the office. I need to call my mother," she said. "It's very important."

Mr. Merlin looked at the clock.

"It's almost time for lunch, Amber Lee," he said. "Can't it wait?"

"No, Mr. Merlin," she said. "It can't wait."

"Well, all right," Mr. Merlin said.

Amber Lee ran out of class.

Noelle looked at Todd.

"I think she knows who we were talking about," Noelle whispered.

"You told the class too much," Todd whispered back.

In just a few minutes, Amber Lee returned to the room.

She smiled at Noelle and Todd.

"I was right. Amber Lee knows the blond hairs belong to Preston," Noelle whispered to Todd. "She's going to try to solve the mystery before we do!"

The bell for lunch finally rang.

Noelle and Todd headed for the cafeteria.

While they were getting their trays, they looked around for Preston.

Finally, Noelle saw him on the other side of the cafeteria.

Amber Lee was whispering something in his ear.

When she finished, she handed him a baseball cap.

Preston put it on his head.

"Hey! That's my baseball cap!" Todd said. "Amber Lee gave him my baseball cap!"

"I don't think that's yours," Noelle said.

"I think it's one that looks like yours."

She thought for a minute.

"That's strange.

Why would Amber Lee give him a cap if she wanted to get one of his hairs?"

"Maybe she already has one of his hairs," Todd said.

"That's it!" Noelle said.

"That's why Amber Lee went to the principal's office, too.

"She called her mother to bring her a baseball cap so she could give it to Preston.

"None of his hairs will fall onto my tomatoes if he's wearing that cap."

"I can't believe it!" Todd said.

"She'll have one of his hairs, and we won't.

"Now she'll be able to solve the mystery."

"Maybe. Maybe not," Noelle said.

"She doesn't have the hairs from Mrs. Ruston's farm.

"She doesn't have the hair from her tomato, either. And she doesn't have the evidence we do."

They found a place to sit down.

But Noelle kept looking at Amber Lee and Preston.

All the kids sitting around them were giving Preston their tomatoes.

"He did it! I know he did! Everything fits!"

Noelle said. "He has long, blond hair, and he loves tomatoes."

"But we'll never be able to prove it if we can't get one of his hairs," Todd said.

Suddenly, Noelle looked over at Todd.

"Did you wear your baseball cap to school today?" she said.

"Yes," Todd said. "It's in the coatroom."

"Go get it!" Noelle said. "I've got a plan!"

Chapter Ten

Todd got his baseball cap from the coatroom and hurried back to the cafeteria.

"Did anything happen while I was gone?" he asked Noelle.

"Yes, it did," Noelle said. "Mrs. Jenkins told Preston to take off his cap."

Todd looked.

"Well, why is he still wearing it?" he asked.

"Because Amber Lee whispered something to Mrs. Jenkins," Noelle said. "Maybe she told her Preston needed to wear it because he was losing his hair."

"That's not fair," Todd said.

"Never mind. Just give me your cap," Noelle said. "We need to work fast."

Noelle put the cap behind her back.

They started toward the table where Preston was sitting.

Amber Lee saw them coming.

She gave them a suspicious look.

When they reached the table, Noelle grabbed the cap off Preston's head.

"That's a great cap, Preston!" she said. "I wish I had one like it."

"Hey, stop that!" Preston cried.

"Noelle! Put that cap back on his head!" Amber Lee shouted. "You're not going to get Preston in trouble!"

"Okay. Okay," Noelle said.

Quickly, she switched caps and put Todd's on Preston's head.

Then she headed toward the cafeteria door.

Todd was right behind her.

"What was that all about?" he asked.

Noelle grinned.

"Didn't you see me?

"I switched caps.

"Preston is now wearing your cap.

"I have the one that was on his head."

Todd looked puzzled. "Why did you give

him *my* cap?" he demanded.

"Because I think this cap will have some of his hairs inside it," Noelle explained.

"We'll take it to Dr. Smiley's house after school and find out for sure.

"We don't have to worry about Amber Lee solving the mystery, either."

"Why?" Todd asked.

"She doesn't want Preston to get in trouble, that's why," Noelle said. "She gave him the cap so *we* couldn't get some of his hair.

"She must really like him a lot."

When school was out, Noelle and Todd headed to Dr. Smiley's house.

Noelle told her what she had done.

"Well, let's examine the evidence and see what we can find," Dr. Smiley said.

They went downstairs to her basement laboratory.

Dr. Smiley used a large magnifying glass to examine the inside of the baseball cap.

"There are a couple of long, blond hairs here," she said.

She picked them out with a pair of tweezers.

She laid them on top of a glass counter.

"We need to compare one of these hairs with the ones we found at Mrs. Ruston's farm and on Amber Lee's tomato," Noelle said.

"Right," Dr. Smiley said.

She prepared a slide with the three hairs.

She looked at it under a microscope.

She smiled at Noelle and Todd.

"Take a look," she said.

Noelle looked.

Todd looked.

"They look the same to me," Noelle said.

"Me, too," Todd said.

"I agree," Dr. Smiley said. "I think all three hairs belong to Preston Edwards."

The next morning, Noelle and Todd presented their evidence to Mr. Merlin.

Then they went with him to the principal's office.

Mrs. Jenkins called Preston and Mrs. Ruston to her office.

Preston was still wearing the baseball cap.

"I know why I'm here," he said. "I'm sorry I did it."

He explained that his parents were allergic to tomatoes, so they never had them in the house.

But Preston loved tomatoes.

He couldn't get enough of them to eat.

He couldn't resist the fat, juicy tomatoes in Mrs. Ruston's garden.

He got scared that someone would find out, so he made it look like a dog had been digging in the garden.

He looked at Noelle and Todd.

"I didn't know Mr. Merlin's Third-Grade Detectives were so good at solving mysteries."

"Well, they are," Mr. Merlin said.

Mrs. Jenkins turned to Mrs. Ruston.

"What should we do now?" she asked.

"If Preston's parents will agree to let him work for me at the farm on weekends, I'll drop the charges," Mrs. Ruston said.

"They'll agree," Preston said.

"You won't get paid any money for doing this, Preston, because it'll be part of your punishment," Mrs. Ruston said, "but if you do a good job,

I'll give you all the tomatoes you can eat."

"You can count on me," Preston said.

Mrs. Ruston turned to Noelle. "I'm sorry I thought Rover did it," she said. "I'll be by this evening to apologize to him."

Noelle grinned.

"Rover will be waiting for you," she said.

Can You Break the Code?

Here's a message in code that will tell you more about what police know about hairs:

```
JIROVX  VTH  AXRR
DNXANXL  T  NTOL  VTSX
YLIS  ANX  NXTW,  UXTLW,
XFXULID, XFXRTMN,
TLSJOA,  IL  IANXL  JRTVXM
IH  T  JXLMIH'M  UIWF.
```

To decode it, use the split alphabet code that Mr. Merlin gave his class. (HINT: Split it, rewrite it, and split it again.)

If you had trouble decoding this secret message, you should write out the regular alphabet in a single line:

ABCDEFGHIJKLMNOPQRSTUWXYZ

Split it:

ABCDEFGHIJKLM
NOPQRSTUVWXYZ

Rewrite it from top to bottom in a single line:

ANBOCPDQERFSGTHUIVJWKXLYMZ

Split it again:

ANBOCPDQERFSG
THUIVJWKXLYMZ

(See: note above)

Use this split alphabet to decode your secret message:

Answer:

Police can tell whether a hair came from the head, beard, eyebrow, eyelash, armpit, or other places on a person's body.